STO

12/07

FRIENDS OF ACPL

O9-ABI-249

To my wonderful family, especially Anne Terrill, who started it all.
With a barn-sized thanks to Heidi Kilgras,
Kate Klimo, and Peter Terrill.
—B.T.

In loving memory of my father, Dennis,
who showed me the true meaning of Christmas,
and to my mother, Deanna, who still does.
—G.N.

Text copyright © 2007 by Beth Terrill
Illustrations copyright © 2007 by Greg Newbold

All rights reserved.
Published in the United States by Random House Children's Books, a division of Random House, Inc., New York.

RANDOM HOUSE and colophon are registered trademarks of Random House, Inc.

www.randomhouse.com/kids

Educators and librarians, for a variety of teaching tools, visit us at www.randomhouse.com/teachers

Library of Congress Cataloging-in-Publication Data
Terrill, Beth.
The barnyard night before Christmas / by Beth Terrill ; illustrated by Greg Newbold. — 1st ed.
p. cm.
ISBN 978-0-375-83682-4 (trade) — ISBN 978-0-375-93682-1 (lib. bdg.)
1. Christmas—Juvenile poetry. 2. Santa Claus—Juvenile poetry. 3. Children's poetry, American. I. Newbold, Greg
(Gregory L.), ill. II. Title.
PS3570.E6935B37 2007
811'.54—dc22
2006035615

Printed in China

10 9 8 7 6 5 4 3 2 1

First Edition

The Barnyard
Night Before Christmas

By Beth Terrill
Illustrated by Greg Newbold

Random House New York

'Twas the night before Christmas, when down on the farm
Not a creature was sleeping inside the old barn.
Though the mouse wrote a letter to Santa with care,
None thought that St. Nicholas would ever stop there.

The horse, he was pouting atop his straw bed.
No visions of sugar cubes pranced in his head.
The duck and the chicken, the dog and the sheep,
Had given up hope for a long winter's sleep.

With no peace in the barn, they sang not a song,
For the animals, this year, were not getting along.

Then outside the barn, there arose such a clatter!
The animals rushed out to see what was the matter.
Who made that racket? What made such a sound?
While the duck blamed the others, the pig sniffed around.

As the pig searched for clues on that cold winter's night,
The others started a big snowball fight—
When what to their wondering eyes should appear
But that jolly St. Nicholas *without* his reindeer.

"Too much sweet Christmas pudding!" they heard Santa say.
"My reindeer can't fly me the rest of the way.
I can't bring my gifts to the girls and the boys
Unless *someone* can help me deliver their toys."

The horse said, "Of course *I* can carry your sleigh."
"But Santa needs eight—" the dog started to say.
"Let's paddle the sleigh!" quacked the duck. "It might float."
"Baaa haaa!" laughed the sheep. "It's a sleigh, not a boat!"

The animals argued as Santa lost hope,
Till Pip, the mouse, found balloons and some rope.

"Balloons!" oinked the pig. "Hey, the whole farm could fly!
Because it's for Santa, let's give it a try."
"Who made the *pi-i-i-ig* boss?" the goat said with a bleat.
But when Santa *ho-ho*'d, the group jumped to their feet.

With balloons round each belly in red, green, and blue,
The animals started to float, two by two.

Squawking and baaaing, the animals, they came.
Santa whistled and shouted and called them by name:
"Now, Bessie! Now, Billy! Now, Bingo! Now, Piggy!
On, Lambsy! On, Trigger! On, Quacker and Chickie."

3 1833 05335 1414

And laying his finger aside of his nose,

Up, up, Santa Claus with those animals rose.

"To the top of the barn! To the top of the stall!

Now dash away! Dash away—*DON'T CRASH!!!*—away, all!"

Those animals flew high o'er the new-fallen snow,

Till the houses and farms looked like toys down below.

But, nipping and kicking—all wanting their way—
They bounced Santa's presents right out of the sleigh.
There fell a great hush—not a soul made a sound
As they watched all the presents fall down toward the ground.

But that brave little pig, he split from the pack—
Dove down through the air and reached out for that sack!
Pip tied Piggy's rope so his fall could be stopped!

But then the rope snapped—so that poor Piggy dropped!

As Piggy fell down, he let out a yelp! . . .

And those animals answered—they rushed in to help.

With a peck-peck from Chickie, two balloons went *POP! POP!*
And Billy and Bingo . . . *they* started to drop!
On down to that pig and those presents they flew,
And woolly old Lambsy knew just what to do!

Bessie knitted wool ropes, which Pip quickly tied.
And Trigger, he lassoed three friends in one try.
With a cluck and a grunt and a baaa, moo, and neigh,
They pulled Santa's presents back up to the sleigh.
The dolls, trains, and baseballs that fell from the sack
Were caught quick by Quacker, who flew them right back.

On down to each housetop the farm friends, they flew
With the sleigh full of toys, and Santa Claus, too.
And then, in a twinkling, was heard on each roof
The stomping and stumbling of each claw, paw, and hoof.

All the boys' and girls' stockings were soon filled with care,
For, thanks to the animals, St. Nicholas was there.

Back to the farm they flew, lively and quick.
They smiled at each other, gave high hooves to St. Nick.
The reindeer, well rested, took back their old places.
The barn mouse had never seen happier faces.

Santa winked at sweet Pip, then opened his pack—
One last bundle of gifts he had worn on his back.

There were oats, corn, and clover; toys brimming with charm;
Matching earmuffs and blankets, and bells for the farm.
"Who'll fly with me next year?" he asked of the crew.
The pig raised his trotter, and Pip squeaked, "Me too!"

Santa sprang to his sleigh, to his team gave a shout,
And flew over each upraised beak, muzzle, and snout.

And they heard Santa say, ere he flew out of sight,
"Happy barnyard to all, and to all a good night!"

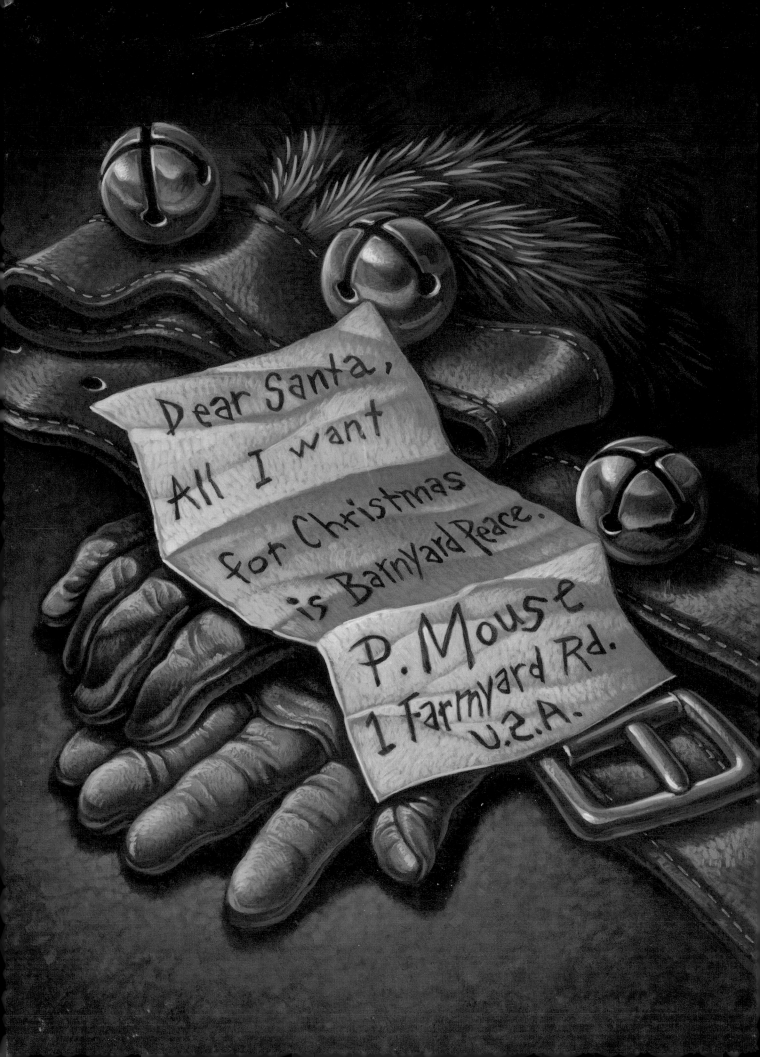